For my amazing family who have given me unconditional support throughout this entire process.

And of course….. for the real Stinkerton Mcpoo!

STINKERTON MCPOO GOES EXPLORING by **STEPHEN HODGKINSON-SOTO**. Published by **ASAG PUBLISHING**

www.stinkertonmcpoo.com

ISBN-13: 978-1-7399052-0-0

The Stinkerton McPoo Dog Series

Stinkerton
McPoo

Goes Exploring

This is the tale of Stinkerton McPoo.
The finest of dogs, and the friendliest too.
Now you may be asking, "But what's with that name?"
To call a dog Stinkerton seems like a shame.

Stinkerton lives with a family that's ace.
There's Papi, and Daddy, and AJ, and Grace.
McPoo and the family all fit like a glove,
And despite the bad smells, they fell quickly in love.

One sunny day Miss McPoo went exploring.
(The view from the garden was terribly boring).
She thought to herself here's my chance to escape –
Someone's forgotten to close the back gate!

Freedom at last, now where should I roam?
She ran through the village a long way from home.
Suddenly, Stinkerton stopped in her tracks.
As her nose caught the smell of some glorious snacks.

In through the door of the Butcher's she trotted.
Sneaking in back of the counter unspotted.
Grabbing some sausages down from a plate.
She rushed for the door just a little too late.

The Butcher was yelling, "Don't let that dog past!",
When out of her rear came a terrible blast!
In all the confusion, she made her escape,
Taking the sausages (leaving the plate).

On down the road she continued to race.
The Butcher and customers all giving chase.
More and more people were starting to run,
And Stinkerton thought this was marvelous fun!

The Post Person's name was Veronica Snail.
And she rounded the corner, her arms full of mail.
Stinkerton shoved her way past without care,
And all of the letters flew up in the air.

The crowd behind Stinkerton started to grow.
With all of those people, she dared not go slow.
She aimed for a hedge,
Which she cleared with a hop,
And sausages dangling, entered a shop.

The Shopkeeper, snoring, was taking a break.
But with all the commotion, he startled awake.
He tried to make sense of the scene through his fog.
"Why are those people all chasing that dog?"

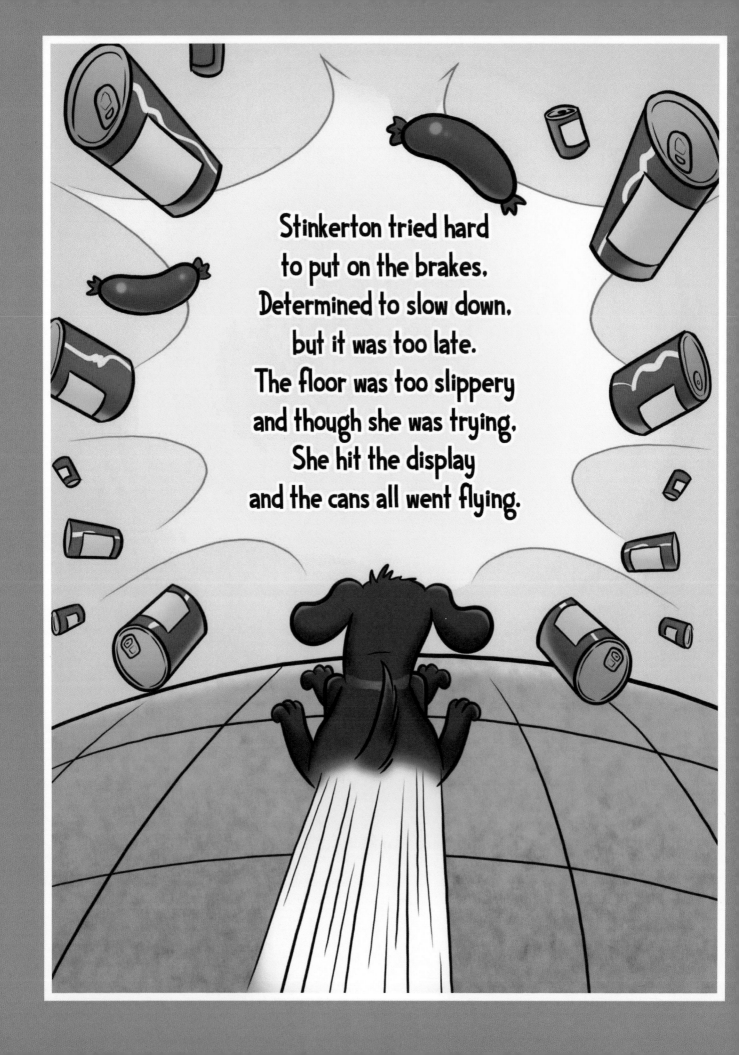

Stinkerton thought she had run out of luck.
The exits were few and she just might be stuck.
The crowd looming over her yelled,
"Now we got'em!",
When something quite stinky
squeaked out of her bottom!

As the gas cloud was clearing, McPoo snuck out back.
She was thinking she needed a safe place to snack.
"After her!" shouted the frustrated crowd.
"Stealing those sausages isn't allowed!"

On down the high street Miss Stinkerton fled.
Straight through the traffic lights (though they were red).
Now there were dozens of people pursuing.
Didn't they have better things to be doing?

Once more on the run. Miss McPoo headed right.
The crowd that was chasing her made such a sight.
McPoo had a plan (she was nobody's fool).
She ran down the High Street and right into school.

Inside the classroom, Miss Butters was saying,
"Open your books, please be quiet, stop playing!"
AJ and Gracie were sitting up front,
When the people all tumbled inside on their hunt.

Once more came that gas in a gigantic plume.
Everyone rushed out and emptied the room.
Stinkerton looked for a way to escape.
Inside her mind was a plan taking shape.

That's when it hit her, she let out a bark,
And jumped out the window
to head to the park.
But as she snuck out,
something tickled her nose,
Tipped off by the sneeze
someone yelled, "There she goes!"

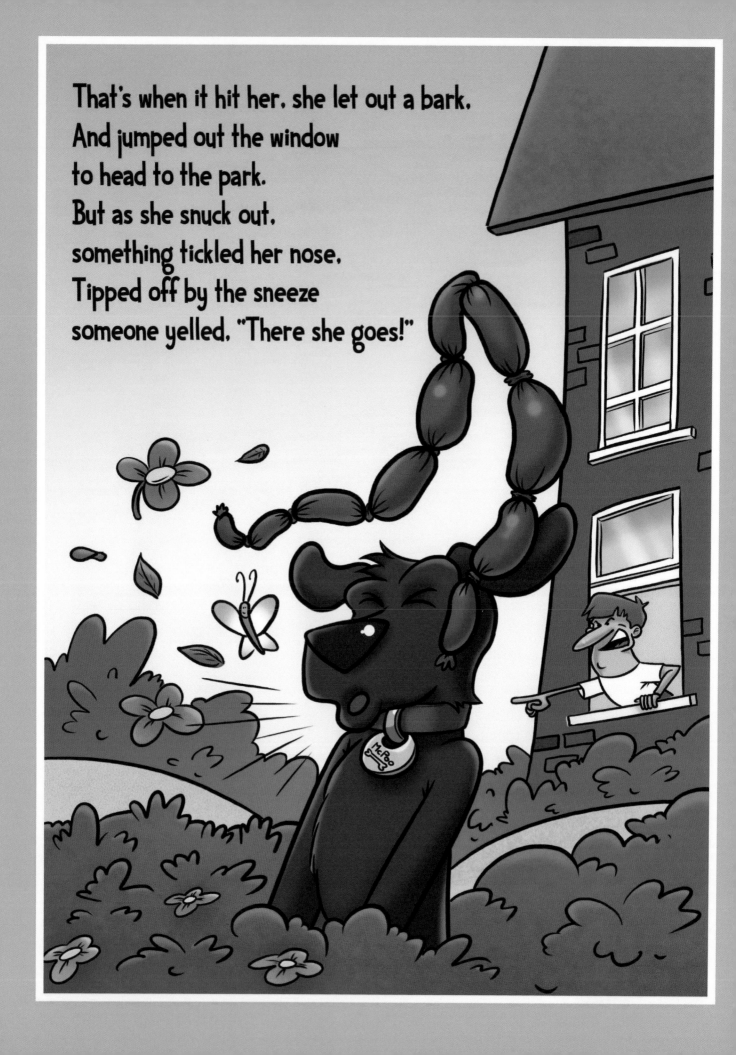

Again she was running pursued by the mob.
Staying ahead of them proved quite a job.
The park had a pond that's a popular place.
It was there that McPoo had decided to race.

As she drew near, she was practically flying,
But next to the pond, a young girl sat, crying.
"My kitten has floated away on that log!
"It drifted away while I looked for a frog!"

McPoo didn't hesitate, not for one second.
"I'll save the kitten from drowning," she reckoned.
Dropping the sausages, she started to swim.
She soon reached the kitten
whose face looked quite grim.

McPoo pushed the log and the kitten to shore.
Cheering, the crowd gave an almighty roar.
"Oh thank you for saving my kitten from drowning!"
(Even the Butcher was no longer frowning).

"I think you have earned these for saving that kitten."
McPoo kept the sausages (all slightly bitten).
Again from the crowd came a thunderous cheer,
And Stinkerton knew she had nothing to fear.

You may now be thinking, this must be the end,
But one more thing happened I just can't defend.
Just as the townsfolk were walking right past,
Stinkerton offered up one final blast...

Other Books in the Series

Stinkerton Mcpoo Goes Exploring Coloring Book

(available on Amazon)

A Note from the Author

I sincerely hope that you and your little ones have enjoyed reading this book. In this day and age, it is almost impossible for self-publishing authors such as myself to survive without the use of Amazon. It would help me out tremendously if you could take the time to leave a short review.

Positive reviews are the key to helping a book stand out in the ever-increasing competitive world of online self-publishing. Thank you!

If you would like to find out more about the real Stinkerton Mcpoo, receive exclusive content, or find out about upcoming releases – please visit the website at www.stinkertonmcpoo.com

About The Author

Stephen Hodgkinson-Soto lives in the East Midlands of England. He has been with his husband Antonio since 2009. Having met while living in California, they moved to the UK in 2017. They have two children named AJ & Graciela, and two dogs named Fia & Esperanza. Fia is the inspiration behind this book series, and although lovely company, is known as "Stinkerton McPoo" - and for good reason!

While new to writing, Stephen has had the idea for the Stinkerton McPoo books for a while, and ready to explore other creative outlets, he has decided to pursue his dream of becoming a best-selling author.

 He hopes you enjoy reading this book as much as he has enjoyed writing it, and he's excited to announce his plans for many more books in the Stinkerton McPoo series.

Printed in Great Britain
by Amazon